" WISHING YOU SWE.
- GAMPERS -

MW00978492

THE GAMPERSTONE

A FEEL GOOD STORY

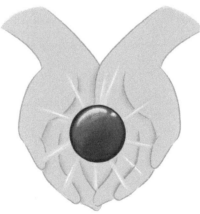

MARTIN "GAMPERS" TKACHUK

 FriesenPress

One Printers Way
Altona, MB R0G 0B0
Canada

www.friesenpress.com

Copyright © 2023 by Martin "Gampers" Tkachuk
First Edition — 2023

Illustrations by Charlemagne B. Claros

All rights reserved.

No part of this publication may be reproduced in any form, or by any means, electronic or mechanical, including photocopying, recording, or any information browsing, storage, or retrieval system, without permission in writing from FriesenPress.

Thank you Nancy. I could not do this without your support and expertise.

Thank you Kayla Lang and Friesen Press, for the editing support and patience in this project.

Thank you Charlemagne for your artwork. It sets the mood of the story.

And, thank you all, my family, Jillian, London, Wolfe and Boris for inspiring this story in me.

ISBN
978-1-03-915223-6 (Hardcover)
978-1-03-915222-9 (Paperback)
978-1-03-915224-3 (eBook)

1. Juvenile Fiction, Bedtime & Dreams

Distributed to the trade by The Ingram Book Company

For London and Wolfe,
Inspired in my heart by Jillian

London and Wolfe are going to Gramma and Gampers house for the weekend. They're bringing their dog, Boris, with them.

They love Gramma and Gampers' house because they love to play, and Gramma and Gampers like to play too! Playing makes London and Wolfe feel happy and safe.

London and Wolfe both have wonderful imaginations! When they get to Gramma and Gampers' house, they play dress-up and pretend to be their favourite characters.

London loves being a princess. She dresses up as a beautiful snow queen and rules over Wolfe and Boris with love and kindness.

She then transforms into a fun mermaid and goes on adventures under the sea. But Wolfe wants to play something else.

Wolfe likes cars and trains, so he fetches his favourite ones from his backpack. He pretends they go really fast, and that makes him laugh!

Later, London and Wolfe bake cookies with Gramma. Baking with Gramma is always fun, and Gramma enjoys her special time with London and Wolfe.

While they're in the kitchen, Gampers heads out to his workshop. Gampers likes to make things out of wood. He makes all kinds of things, like tables and shelves, and he makes fun stuff too!

Today, he has some leftover wood, but it's too beautiful to throw away. Using the tools in his shop, Gampers carves and sands the wood until it becomes round, smooth, and shiny.

When it's finished, it looks like a river rock used for skipping stones across the water. Or maybe a small wheel for a toy car or truck. Gampers smiles. Or maybe it will be part of a fantastic spaceship or boat...

Gampers feels good holding the smooth, shiny, and round piece of wood in his hands. It makes him feel happy. Gampers thinks of London and Wolfe. Maybe the Gamperstone would make the kidlets (as Gampers likes to call them) feel happy too!

He wonders if holding the Gamperstone might be a good way for them to think of all the good things they love, whenever they're having a "not so good" kind of day.

So, Gampers decides to see if the children like the Gamperstone as much as he does. He lovingly makes another one, so both kidlets can have one.

In the kitchen, Gampers hands one Gamperstone to London and one to Wolfe. The kidlets' faces light up with wonder and awe. They love the Gamperstones! Gampers is very pleased. He tells them what each one means to him.

"It is not magical, but it can be very powerful.

Keep it by your bedside or under your pillow.

Carry it with you if you must.

Hold it in your hands when you are sad, lonely, lost, or afraid, or if you just need to calm down.

Feel the love it holds.

Hold it and think of all
the people you love
and all the people who
love you.

Think of kindness,
cuddles, and hugs that
calm your heart."

Gramma finishes cleaning the kitchen while London and Wolfe chase Gampers around the house. It's a great way to play and have more fun.

After a few minutes, Gampers gets too far ahead of them and hides. When they get close to his hiding spot, he jumps out and surprises them!

The kidlets jump on Gramma's bed, laughing and screaming, then hide in the pillows.

But Gampers finds them, and they have a pillow fight, laughing and squealing in delight.

At the end of the day, when the fun and adventures are over, it's time to settle down for bed.

Gramma reads a bedtime story as the kidlets snuggle in with Gampers. After hugs and kisses, London and Wolfe are ready to sleep.

But London and Wolfe find it hard to fall asleep. They think about their day. Not all of it was fun, like when heads got bumped or elbows got scratched. That hurt!

London still felt bad that she had dropped the cookie dough on the floor while baking with Gramma.

Wolfe was thinking about the bossy name he'd called London while they were playing dress-up. He thought "something else" might be coming to punish him.

Wolfe saw something move across the wall. It was just a shadow, right? It wasn't ... something else.
Then he heard a creaking sound. Shadows can't make noise, can they?
"Who's there?"

Then London and Wolfe remember their GAMPERSTONES!

They find the Gamperstones under their pillows and hold them, thinking about all the things they really love.

They think about all the people they love ... who love them back and make them feel safe.

Mommy and Daddy, cuddles and hugs, car rides, and the beach.

Gramma and Gampers, baking, playing in the pool and in the yard, and snuggling on the sofa.

Nana and Poppa, Boris, playing and laughing with cousins, besties, and aunts and uncles.

Holding the Gamperstones helps the kidlets calm down and feel safe again. Slowly, London and Wolfe drift into restful sleep— sleep filled with sweet dreams.

The next morning, feeling refreshed, London and Wolfe run to the kitchen to tell Gramma and Gampers all about their happy dreams with the Gamperstones.

Gampers wonders if other children could find their own Gamperstones.

A Gamperstone can be anything that feels good to hold in your hands. It can be a pretty rock, an ornament, or a small toy. It can be anything that is comforting, feels good to touch, and helps you think positive thoughts about the people you love and who love you back.

Reminding ourselves to think positive thoughts of love and kindness can help us overcome our fears—our "something else."

Just like Gampers, Gamperstones are filled with love and kindness.

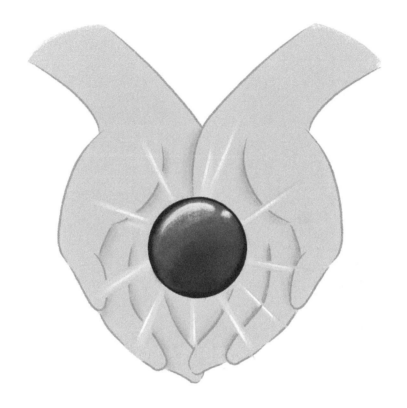

They are not magical, but they can be very powerful.

About the Author

THE GAMPERSTONE is based on Martin Tkachuk's real-life experience of wanting to find a way to help calm his grandchildren when they become anxious. Being a woodwork hobbyist, Tkachuk created Gamperstones for his grandchildren so they could overcome their anxiety by remembering all the good things in their lives. In his spare time, Tkachuk enjoys fishing, camping, and travelling with his family. He lives with his wife in Niagara Falls, Ontario, where they are enjoying being retired.

CPSIA information can be obtained
at www.ICGtesting.com
Printed in the USA
JSHW071057270223
38242JS00003B/11